Archaeological Adviser BARRY CUNLIFFE

Series Editor JOHN W HEDGES

CATVS

A CHILD IN ROMAN BRITAIN AD 80

Written by TERESA WOODBRIDGE

Illustrated by D E WALDUCK

For James

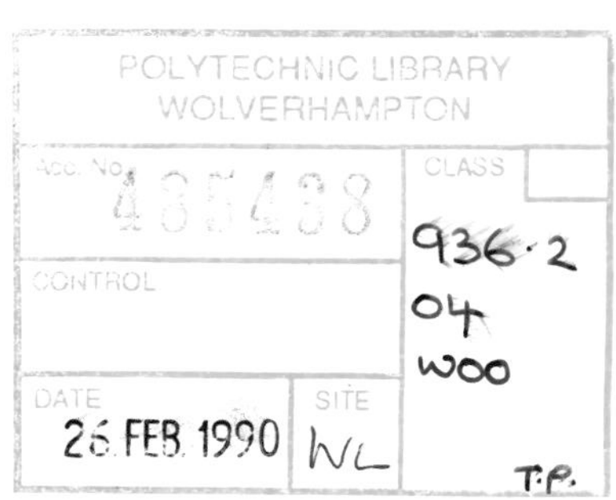

TEMPVS REPARATVM ARCHAEOLOGICAL AND HISTORICAL ASSOCIATES LTD

— ***Journeys Through Time*** —

First published 1989 by TEMPVS REPARATVM Archaeological and Historical Associates Ltd.

ISBN 1 871314 01 1

This and others in the Journeys Through Time series are available from booksellers and, direct, from 4 Cyprus Terrace, Oxford OX2 8AT.

Typeset by The Bocardo Press
Printed by Information Press

What was it like to be a British boy living in the wilds of the Sussex Downs in the years immediately after the Roman conquest of Britain? You might have grown up, like our hero Catus, totally unaware of the garish villas and towns sprung up on the coastal plains — unaware, that is, until suddenly you were thrust among them as a slave working in the kitchens of the great palace of Fishbourne and later visiting the sanctuary of the goddess Sulis Minerva at Bath. How would you have reacted — would you have welcomed the invaders or rebelled against them? This was the problem that Catus had to face.

We know a lot about Britain at this time. The palace at Fishbourne and the Roman temple and baths at Bath have been excavated and can now be visited. The mosaics of the palace and the altar of the temple shown in our picture story are there for you to see. Around the wealth of detail recovered by archaeologists Teresa Woodbridge has woven an exciting story that, together with D E Walduck's vivid illustrations, brings Roman Britain to life again. When you have read the book, why not try to retrace some of Catus' journey?

Barry Cunliffe

Professor Barry Cunliffe
Institute of Archaeology, Oxford, April 1989

IT WAS SAMAIN when Catus heard the news. The feast to celebrate the beginning of the new year was his favourite time, for it was then there was an end to the summer's toil. He knew the summer had been a bad one; the rains had come at the wrong time, the cow had sickened and died, and there had been little enough grass to feed the sheep in the last, cruelly hot months of the season. But now it was ended and it was time to make merry. The women had braided their hair and darkened their lips and cheeks with elderberry juice. All the villagers were seated round the fire, feasting and drinking strong drink — home brewed ale and mead. The sheep had been herded inside the village for the winter. Some had been killed and their skins stretched out on frames, the meat salted and hung up to dry. The fattest had been chosen for this feast, and the women had roasted them over the fire. Now the villagers were wiping the grease from their hands and lips before the storytelling began.

"Catus!" His father pulled him aside, out of the fire's warm glow. It was too dark to see his face properly, but Catus caught the sickly smell of mead on his breath. "We've had a piece of luck," he continued unsteadily. "There's a job for you, at the Palace by the sea. You'll have food for your belly, a warm place to sleep. Maybe you'll make something of yourself. We can't give you much here, and with the new baby coming . . ."

Distantly Catus could hear his father's voice going on, explaining, excusing himself, threatening, but he heard no more. Nor could he look up at his father's face, blurred by the drink and the night's shadows. Hot tears pricked his eyes. He knew what a job at the Palace meant. He understood now why his father had come back from town with a bag full of coins. He had been sold as a slave!

The first weeks of working in the busy kitchen at the Palace were like a bad dream. There was so much that was new — the people, the work, the Palace itself and, above all, the language. Few of the other slaves cared to speak to Catus in his own tongue, even those who, like him, had been born in these parts. The cook himself was from Gaul, and Catus often had a hard job understanding what was wanted of him. Only a few short miles from his village, but it seemed a different world.

Up before dawn, his job was to see to the fires, grind corn for the bread, fetch and carry water, run errands for the Palace cook . . . the work was never ending. The King's household ate a simple meal at daybreak — just porridge or bread and watered wine, with sometimes a little honey and an apple or a pear for the children. At midday cold meat or dried fish was served with salad and bread and fruit. It was at the end of the day that the King and his family had their main meal, after they had offered some little cakes to the household gods. And what a meal it was!

When he had a spare moment Catus would watch in amazement as the cook prepared the food. As a first course there would be hard-boiled eggs, a bowl of olives or shellfish; and this was followed by sometimes as many as seven courses of meat and fish. Many of the foods were strange to Catus. There were figs, dates, dried grapes and rare spices from over the seas; and even the fish, meats and fruits of his own country were prepared in a new way, using olive oil, honey and strong fishy liquamen in the cooking. After the meat there were fruit, nuts, honey cakes and pastries, all washed down with blood-red wine from over the seas. It was Catus's job to pile the heaps of fragrant, steaming food into the endless red-glazed bowls that were carried to the table, but it was better when the bowls returned to be washed, some still half full, and he could satisfy his hunger with the scraps.

Catus liked it best when he was sent to the kitchen garden for vegetables or fresh herbs. There was no-one there to shout at him or bully him, and he could escape from the smoky kitchen and breathe some fresh air for a few moments. It was there, one morning in that first winter at the Palace, that he met the King.

The kitchen boy was on his knees by a rosemary bush, picking shoots, when something soft and sharp leapt on his back. Turning in surprise, he saw a small black kitten crouched on his shoulder. Where could it have come from? Gently he pulled the cat off his shoulder. It wriggled from his grasp and streaked off, its white front paws twinkling, towards the main garden, where the royal family and their guests walked and took the air. Without a thought Catus set off after it; before he knew it he was in the Palace garden and a small boy had joined in the chase. Together they cornered the kitten and Catus placed it in the boy's arms.

Looking up, to his alarm he met the eyes of an old man holding a young girl by the hand. Catus knew at once that this was King Cogidubnus. He had learned enough now to know that this was his Palace, and surely only a king could look so noble, though so old. And the children must be the royal grandchildren — their Greek nursemaid sometimes came to the kitchen for dainties to tempt their appetites, and would stop for a gossip with one or two of the other slaves. So Catus felt he already knew young Lucius and his sister Claudia.

"Thank you for helping my grandson," said Cogidubnus kindly. "Few boys of your age would have done as much. Where is your home?"

"I was born not ten miles from here, in a village on the downs," Catus replied, reddening.

"Then you, like me, were born a Briton," was the King's reply. "What is your name?"

"Catus," the boy managed to stammer out.

"From now on it shall be Catonius, a good Roman name," said King Cogidubnus, and passed on, the two children behind him.

Soon after, Catonius learned he was to have a new job. He now worked in the living rooms of the Palace, where the two royal grandchildren were. The work was lighter than in the kitchen, the rooms warm and comfortable. When he had time the slave boy would spend a few minutes playing with Lucius. The little boy put him in mind of his own brother, who was much the same age.

The girl, Claudia, was nearer Catonius's own age, but she was mostly busy with her lessons, her music or her sewing. Her father and grandfather were anxious for her to learn to be a real Roman lady, and there were whispers that she might find a husband from the Emperor's own household. Like her mother, she spent long hours with her maid painting her face or trying on her different bits of jewellery, but she was still a child at heart.

There were times when the three of them, well out of sight of Lucius's nursemaid or Claudia's tutor, would talk or play together. Their favourite game was hide and seek, though they often played blind man's buff and even leapfrog and tag too.

Claudia it was who taught Catonius to play the jar game, though she was sorry for it afterwards. "You sit on the ground blindfold, and Lucius and I will take it in turns to pinch you or pull your clothes. If you manage to grab one of us — without getting up, mind — then we will take our turn in the jar."

The two royal children spent a merry few minutes tormenting their friend, who never seemed quite quick enough to catch them. At last, however, Catonius roughly caught hold of Claudia's hand just as she was slipping away from him. Off came her precious ring with the green stone, and went spinning across the mosaic floor. The children hunted high and low for it, but in vain.

"Never mind," said Catonius, for Claudia was weeping by now. "When I'm a rich man I'll buy you another!" Claudia's tears turned to tears of laughter at the joke.

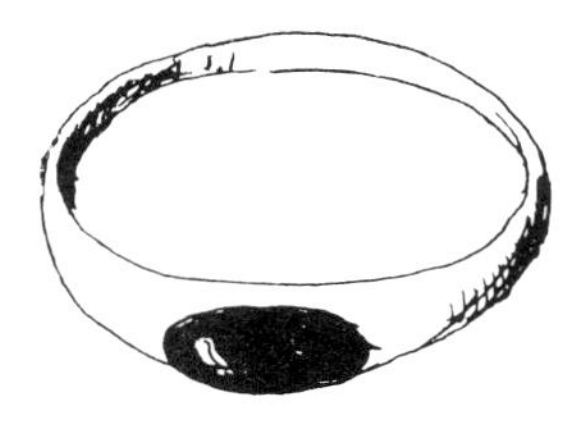

Samain had come and passed again, and it was nearly time for the festival of Belenos. Inside the Palace there were different gods, and the people celebrated different festivals. Catonius often found himself telling Lucius and Claudia about the customs and the stories of his own folk, and about the gods and goddesses of the groves and fields. He told them of the feast of Lug, when the harvest was gathered in, and of the spring festival called Imbolc when the ewes gave milk again. He told them of the swan maidens who became human again at Samain, and of the bonfires built at Beltaine at the beginning of the summer. When he talked about his people his heart often grew sad, yet in some ways the slave boy was happy to live so comfortably in the Palace with his new friends.

Catonius learned that the King was to go on a journey this Beltaine, and that he was to go with him. "Grandfather's poorly," explained Claudia. "He thinks the waters at Aquae Sulis will do him good, and he will sacrifice to Minerva at the Temple."

Aquae Sulis was a good week's journey away, but the days were longer now and the weather mild. For a few days the whole household was busy with preparations for the journey: Catonius began to wonder what sort of place it was, that they had to take so much with them.

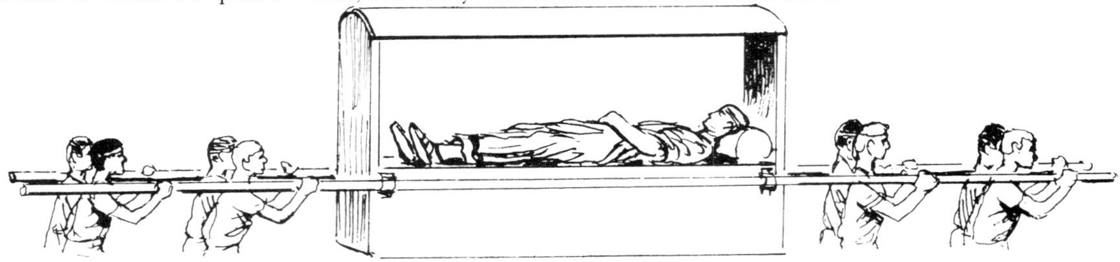

At last the day of the journey dawned. The King was carried out on a lectica, for he was too frail to ride. Around him was an armed guard and his doctor, a clever slave from Greece, was never far away. Carts and wagons followed behind, mules and donkeys with packs on their backs, slaves on foot carrying loads. Catonius felt proud to be part of the household of such a great king.

At the last moment Catonius heard a soft voice calling him and caught sight of Claudia in the shadows. She moved forward and pressed a coin into his hand. "For luck," she whispered, and swiftly fled away.

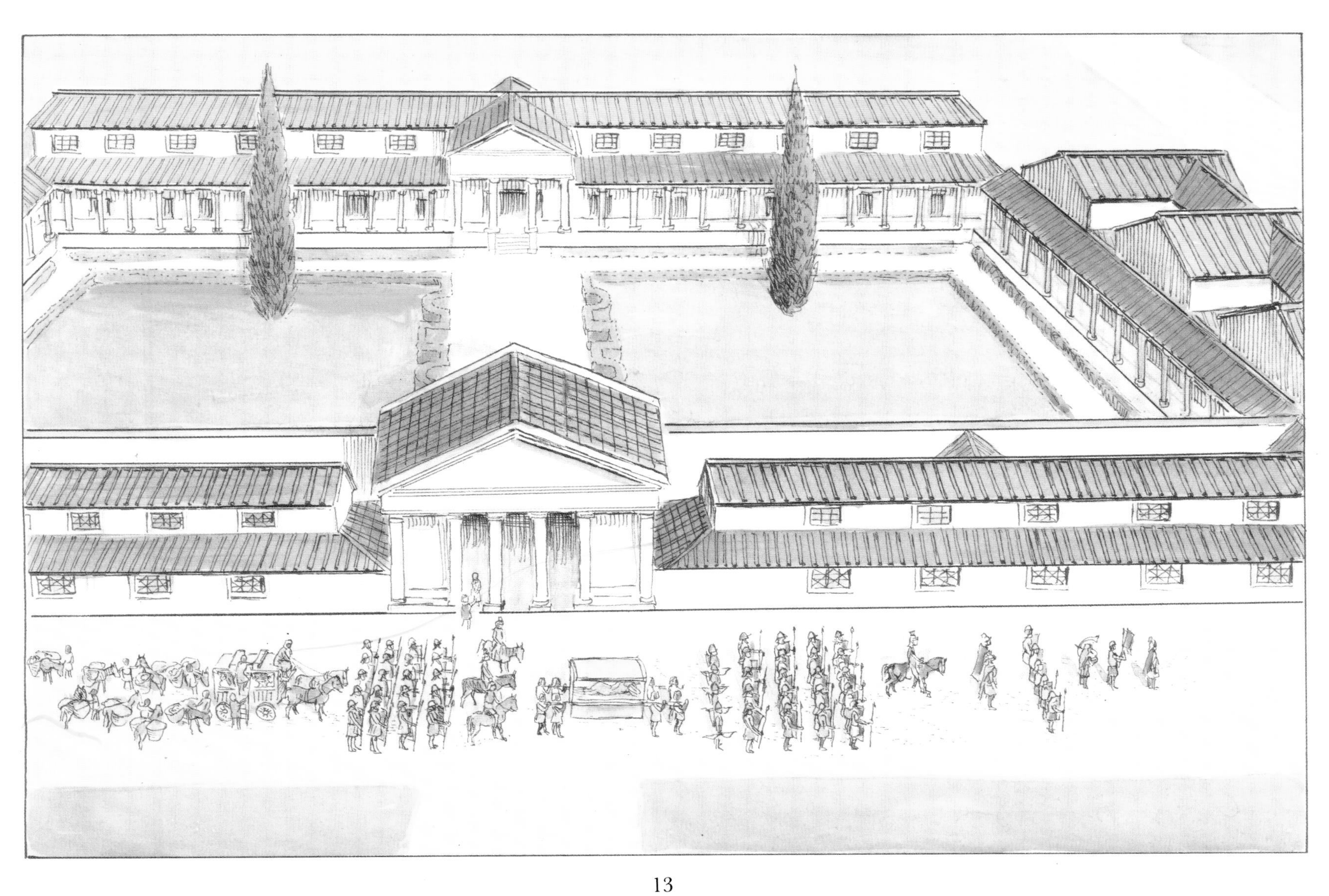

It was some time before Catonius recovered from his surprise and was able to look at the coin that was still clasped tightly in his hand. As a slave, and a young one at that, he had never had a coin of his own before. He thought bitterly of the handful of coins his father had taken in exchange for his son's freedom — how had they been spent, he wondered. On food and shoes for the family, on a new cow, or on jars of sweet wine? Catonius thought he knew the answer. But had his father done so very wrong? Here he was, a member of the King's household, well fed, well dressed, with shoes on his feet and a coin in his hand. And on his way to see the world.

As he marched along with the rest of the procession, leading a difficult mule, Catonius began to dream instead of the shops he could visit in the town and the good things they would have to offer.

They had started when the sun was barely up, and as they went they could see the Beltaine bonfires still glowing on the hills.

It was a two-day journey to Venta, along the broad roads Roman soldiers had built not so very many years before. The way lay straight from hill to hill, and the surface was smooth and flat. Roman soldiers, Catonius had heard, could march thirty miles in one day, but it was slow and painful work to carry an old man in a litter. The air smelt of flowers and new grass, and as the day wore on the sun beat hot on their backs. They passed many travellers on the road; pedlars with their packs, carts loaded with wool and cloth on their way to the port, messengers on horseback, soldiers . . . all moved back respectfully as the King passed by.

It was nearing sunset on the second day when at last they arrived at Venta; mist was rising, and the weary travellers were glad to reach the mansio and lie down.

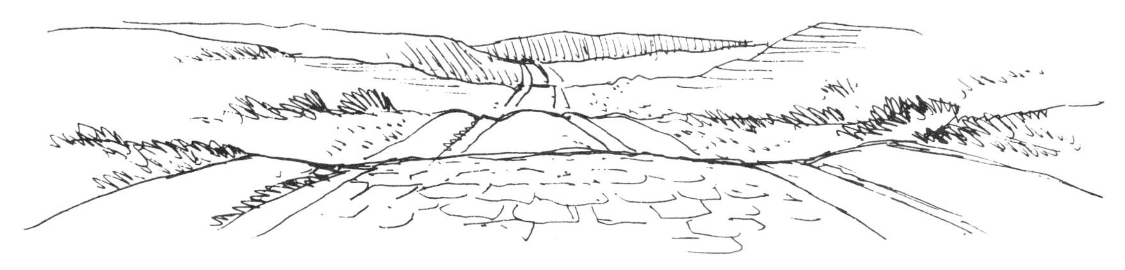

King Cogidubnus was tired by the journey, more tired than he would say, and it was decided to spend the next day in Venta. Catonius was glad to have the chance to see a real town at last. Never in his life had he seen anything more than his village and the Palace, and he set off to see what he could buy in the shops with his precious coin.

At first it was the noise that surprised him. Never before had he seen so many people, and all so busy. At times he had to be careful in case he was knocked flying. Slaves rushed past on their masters' business, officials elbowed him out of the way, busy housewives brushed him aside in their anxiety to get a bargain. There were stalls selling pots, lucky charms, sweetmeats . . . and so many shops! Butchers', bakers', shops selling knives, oil, hot snacks, lengths of cloth . . . everything imaginable. Some, like the bakers, smelt good, but Catonius kept well clear of the shop which sold the liquamen — the smell had been bad enough in the Palace kitchen! The streets too were not all sweet smelling, but Catonius amused himself for hour upon hour walking up and down the streets, marked out in the square pattern of a Roman town. He was enjoying his unexpected holiday.

It was well into the afternoon when Catonius realised that he was due back at the mansio soon and as yet had spent nothing. Round the shops he went again, butchers', bakers', cutlers' . . . and a silversmith with pretty little rings just the size of Claudia's finger. At last he would be able to keep his promise.

For ten minutes or more the boy stood staring at the rings, unable to decide which would best suit her. Once he walked away in despair, but he soon came back again and this time made up his mind to buy a silver ring with a small bird engraved on it, like the bird she kept in the little wicker cage at home. Catonius took the small leather bag from around his neck and pulled out the coin Claudia had given him. Shyly he went up to the shopkeeper and pointed to the ring he wanted, pushing his coin over the counter as he did so. But the silversmith just laughed. "You'll need a deal more than that, lad, to win a girl's heart." And he passed the coin back, still chuckling.

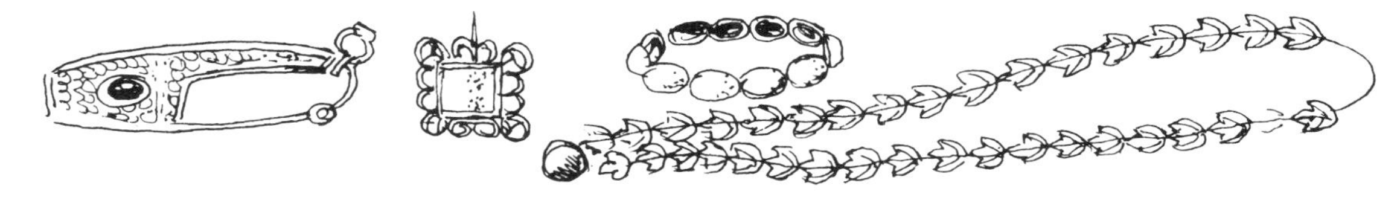

That night, asleep in the mansio, Catonius had a strange dream. An owl was hooting — yet how could there be an owl in the town? When he awoke, tired but restless, he began to be afraid. An owl was a bad sign, surely. It meant ill luck for a journey. And soon they were to cross a wild plain on their way to Aquae Sulis.

Catonius's heart was heavy as they trudged along for the next day or two. The weather had turned sour and the skies were blackening. The king was weaker, so they dared not go too fast. There were no more big towns on the road between Venta and Aquae Sulis, and they were to lodge where they could at roadside inns or at the villas of friends.

Two days out from Venta they entered a bleak and unfriendly landscape. The Roman road passed along an ancient trackway and Catonius seemed to hear the voices of his ancestors hissing in the wind. Away to the north was the ancient Stone Ring where, he had heard, the druids still worshipped; he felt the spirits of the Britons very close at hand.

Storm clouds were gathering now and there was no shelter in sight. A faint sound caught his ear. Surely that was an owl again! But in the daytime? And suddenly there was a new sound, growing steadily nearer. The thunder of horses' hooves! A wild band of native Britons was upon them, coming from every side. Their hair stood back from their faces like horses' manes and their flowing moustaches covered their mouths. They were dressed in brilliant colours, with bright cloaks over their plaid tunics and breeches. Round their necks were heavy metal rings and their swords flashed in their hands.

Catonius watched the fight in horror. The Roman soldiers, quickly recovering from the first alarm, had formed a human wall around the King, using their shields for protection and their long spears to beat back their fearsome attackers. The fight was short but fierce, until finally the wild men gave up the unequal struggle and vanished as suddenly as they had come.

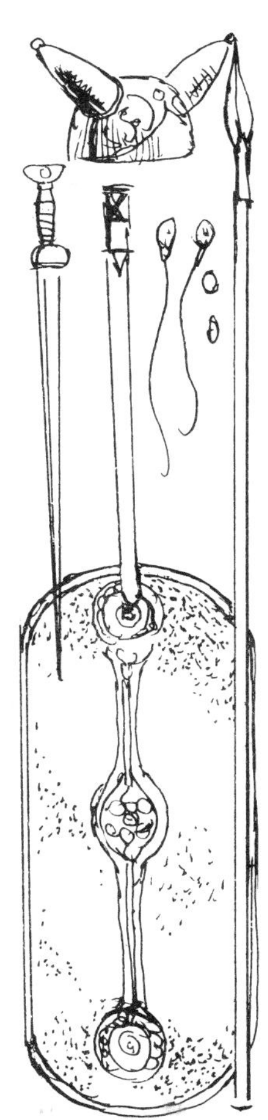

After the attack the party wasted little time on the journey, and were at Aquae Sulis within a few days. But Catonius was full of questions. Who were their attackers? Where had they come from? And why should they want to kill his good King Cogidubnus? Few of the slaves would answer him, but one, Austus by name, satisfied his curiosity. "Those were the Free British," he said. "They remember the days before the Romans took our land and taught us their ways. They hate the Romans — and why not? Why should you, Catus, be a slave in your own land?"

"King Cogidubnus is a Briton, and yet no slave," replied Catonius.

"They reckon Cogidubnus to be worse than the Romans, for he is a traitor. He has sold his own people to the Romans, and apes their manners," was Austus's reply, and after that he would say no more.

Catonius had much to think about. It was months since he had been called by his real name, and he had all but forgotten his own tongue and people. Had his father been right? Was he better off as a slave? He was no longer so sure.

There was little time for thinking in the days that followed. Catonius was needed to help his master in many ways, and there was much to be seen at Aquae Sulis. Every day the King rose a little after dawn — his breakfast of bread and fruit was brought to him in his room in the mansio — and was helped to the Baths. Here he would undress and move from room to room, each warmer than the last, until his weak old body was running with sweat. An attendant would rub him all over with oil and scrape him with a strigil. At last, warm and clean, the King would ease himself into the great pool and swim a few strokes before resting inside.

Catonius had seen baths before at the Palace, but these were quite different. They were huge, and many people travelled long distances to bathe in the healing waters and sacrifice to Sulis Minerva at her temple. Most impressive of all was the sacred spring which came bubbling hot and fierce from the ground. From time to time Catonius could see people throwing offerings to the Goddess into its steaming water.

The King was growing weaker, and his doctor was anxious. Catonius was often asked to help in preparing medicines for his master. He learnt to make soothing draughts from lettuce and parsley, to mix up cooling ointments and to put poultices on the sores on the old man's legs and back.

Sometimes he went up to the hills to gather the herbs his own people used to cure the sick, but nothing seemed to do Cogidubnus any good for long. The only thing that comforted him was to have Catonius sit by him and tell stories or sing songs from his own village. Sometimes the King would correct him on a detail or even tell a completely new story, but most of the time he lay still and silent.

One morning Catonius was surprised to find his master up. "Come round this side, so I may lean on you," the King commanded. "We have tried steaming ourselves, we have tried swimming, we have even drunk the foul-tasting waters. We have followed the physician's advice on everything. And yet we are no better. Today we will try another way. We will sacrifice to Sulis Minerva, and see what the priest has to say."

Catonius helped the King out of the mansio and through the sacred grove to the Temple sacred to Sulis Minerva, where the priest was waiting. Since dawn he had been watching the birds as they flew across the sky, and it was clear from his grave face that the signs boded no good for the King. Cogidubnus, however, showed no sign of fear and walked steadily, though leaning heavily on Catonius's shoulder, behind the priest leading the ritual procession to the altar in front of the Temple. An instant before they halted, the slave boy glanced up and was for an instant terrified by the sight of the huge head on the pediment — with its flowing moustaches and wild hair it had the exact look of one of the Free British who had attacked them. He looked round to the face of the priest, who was examining the entrails of the sheep he had just killed. There was no hope on that priest's face.

After that, it was as though King Cogidubnus no longer cared to be well. His skin became more transparent, his step more unsteady, day by day. He continued to visit the Baths and to follow his doctor's advice, but each day he spent more time with his lawyers and advisers, signing documents and talking to officials. Catonius, fond though he had become of the old King, scarcely noticed this, for a new idea was taking shape in his mind.

Austus had told him the reason that presents, sometimes coins, sometimes beautiful objects, were thrown into the spring. "The Goddess Sulis dwells there," he said. "If you have an enemy she will strike him for you, if you have a wish she will grant it, but you must sweeten her with a gift."

Catonius now had a wish, a wish that grew stronger with each passing day. He had heard his people calling to him on the ridgeway path, he had seen the faces of the Free British who had attacked them on the journey. An owl had hooted — it was a sign. And he had seen the face on the Temple, its eyes boring into him, telling him what to do. He wished to be free!

It was surely right what Austus had told him. The Romans and their minions had taken his land, had made him a slave, taken him from his family. He closed his eyes and tried to picture his family. By some trick the picture would not come, but instead he could see the faces of Lucius and Claudia.

Again he recognised a sign. He had been puzzling what he could give the goddess, and now he knew! With a cry of triumph, he grasped the little leather bag around his neck and with shaking hands drew out the coin that Claudia had given him. He scarcely knew how his trembling legs carried him to the side of the Sacred Spring. "Sulis, make me free!" he whispered, as he flung it right into the middle of the bubbling pool.

That night he packed together his few belongings ready for his escape.

Catonius had planned to slip out of the slaves' quarters late at night, when everyone was asleep. The moon was up, and for the third time he heard an owl hoot. The sound nearly stopped him in his tracks. Was it an unlucky sign, or were the Free British calling him? He could not tell.

As he crept out of the inn, Catonius was startled by the sound of weeping and the unaccustomed smell of incense and burning pine cones. He passed on quickly, and was almost out of sight and sound of the building when a thought struck him. Perhaps his master was worse! He had noticed the doctor's grave face earlier, but had thought little of it, so involved was he in his own plans for escape. Without stopping to think, the boy raced back to the inn and the room where King Cogidubnus lay, pale in death. Around him were his most trusted slaves and his son, who had arrived in Aquae Sulis that very day. The priest too was there, and women, covering their faces in grief and wailing laments.

The doctor noticed the boy standing in the doorway, half in shadow, and stretched out his hand to him. Gently he led him down the corridor, out of the mansio, and to the Sacred Spring. "Catus-Catonius," he began softly, "our master has gone, but he has left us both a gift." He paused a while, watching as the bubbles rose and burst on the surface of the water. "He has made us both freemen, to stay or to leave. I'm too far from my own country, and too long in the tooth, to go back home. But you, you're young. You have the choice. You can go back to your people, or stay at the Palace as a true Roman. I could teach you my craft if you've a mind to it."

In the dark and through his blinding tears the boy could no longer see the fierce face that had glared at him from the pediment of the Temple. Catus-Catonius closed his eyes. Sulis, who had made him free, would show him what was right. Catonius gasped in astonishment. Try as he might, he could no longer see in his mind's eye his family, his little village in the hills.

The faces of Lucius and Claudia were there instead.

THE CELTS

The Celts had already been living in Britain for many years before the Romans invaded them. Some, like King Cogidubnus, were happy to go over to Roman ways and enjoy the new way of life, but others, who are called the Free British in the story, tried to drive the Romans away again. The Celts had their own way of life, their own language, their own gods, their own tribes and their own customs. You will have noticed too that they had different seasons:

Samain (November 1st) was the Celtic New Year festival.

Imbolc was the spring festival when the ewes began to give milk again.

Beltaine or Beltine (the festival of Belenos) was the beginning of summer (May 1st). Bonfires were lit to frighten away evil spirits.

The feast of **Lug** was to celebrate the harvest.

THE ROMANS

The Romans spoke Latin. Here are some Latin words you will find in the story:

Liquamen A strong-tasting (and smelling) sauce made from, among other things, rotted fish.

Lectica We would call this a litter. It is a sort of bed with a cover to keep out sun and rain and with long carrying poles. *See the picture on page 12.*

Mansio An inn in a town where travellers would stay. They might also stay at a roadside inn called a **taverna**.

Strigil Romans didn't use soap. One way of getting clean was to have oil rubbed on their bodies and then pass through the various rooms of the Baths. Each room was a little hotter than the last and it was like a modern Turkish bath or sauna. When they had worked up a good sweat, they or a slave would scrape off the oil, sweat and dirt with a **strigil**. *See the picture on page 20.*

THE JOURNEY

You can see the journey Catonius and Cogidubnus made on the back cover of this book. They started from Fishbourne, near Chichester, which the Romans called Noviomagus Regnensium.

Here are some other Roman names you will find in the story:

Aquae Sulis We know this town as Bath. Sulis was a native goddess who the Celts worshipped there. The Romans called her "Minerva" or "Sulis Minerva" but still called the place "The Waters of Sulis".

Venta Belgarum We call this town **Winchester**. Many towns which were originally Roman end in "—chester" or "—cester" from the Roman word *castrum* meaning "military camp".

THINGS TO READ AND PLACES TO VISIT

Those of you — including teachers — who wish to read more about Roman Britain will find the following books of use:

Britannia by S S Frere (Routledge & Kegan Paul, 3rd edn., 1987).
Roman Britain by T W Potter (British Museum Publications, 1983).
The People of Roman Britain by A Birley (Batsford, 1979).
The Romans: History as Evidence by Mike Corbishley (Kingfisher, 1983).
The Roman World by Mike Corbishley (Kingfisher, 1986).

If you live in or can visit the South of England, you could take a trip to the Roman Palace at Fishbourne, near Chichester, where Catonius worked, and to the Roman Baths at Bath. Wherever you live in the province of Britannia, you will almost certainly be near a Roman site, and your local museum will have pots, jewellery, utensils and coins like the ones in the story.